THE BATTLE
AT
STONE BRIDGE

The Battle at Stone Bridge

ISBN-10: 1945994-14-2
ISBN-13: 978-1-945994-14-2

Edited by Jessica Johnson
interior artwork by Rachel Fast
Tannhauser Press

The Site of the Battle

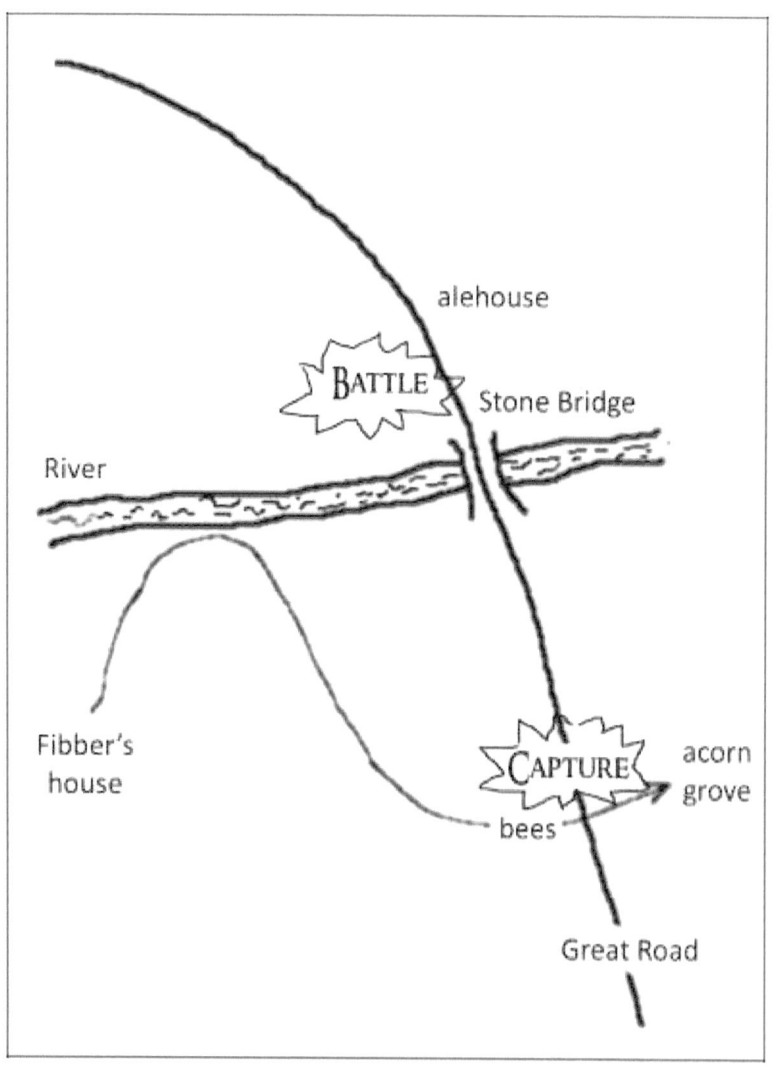

Chapter 1

Tall Tales

ibber Longburrow studied the faces of his kinsmen and neighbors, pressed close around the long trestle table. Fibber's real name was Frederick, but everyone had called him Fibber since he was small.

The alehouse was packed as if every one of his neighbors who lived near the Stone Bridge had stopped in when it got too dark to plow. Most farm cottages were dark inside after sunset, but here in the alehouse, Missus Cowslip built up the fire enough to light even the furthest corners of the room, and she placed candle stubs on every table.

Fibber took a pull from his tankard. He leaned forward and lowered his voice, speaking to anyone who would listen. "It happened not more than a mile from this very spot. There I was, all alone in the woods. There was nothing between me and the wilderness but trees so ancient, they might've been standing there since before this land ever knew a plow.

"A clearing opened up just ahead of me. And what do you think I saw? The largest patch of blackberries I'd ever laid eyes on. As far as I could tell, no one else had discovered it. Not a single berry had been picked. They were as big as grapes, and the branches sagged under their weight. I moved from bush to bush, picking berries and dropping then into my pail as fast as I could pluck them from the branches, while my old dog Blue chased rabbits at the edge of the clearing.

"By late afternoon, the sun was beating down pretty hard. I'd barely made a dent in that magnificent crop of berries, but even so, my pail was just about full. I put it down beside me and picked a few more before calling it a day.

"Blue nuzzled against my leg. I reached down to scratch between his ears, where the fur was thick and soft. Then, on the far side of the clearing, there was a tremendous barking. Blue shot out of the bracken, hard on the heels of an enormous jackrabbit. My hand froze in mid-scratch. If Blue was way over there, whose ears were I scratching?"

Fibber paused and tapped his empty tankard. "Looks like I've run dry again." His neighbor, Robin Stitchwort, dug a coin from his pocket and dropped it on the table. Missus Cowslip, the alewife, came over with a jug and filled Fibber's tankard. He drained the bitter brew she was famous for in a single draft and held out his tankard for another.

He wiped the foam from his mouth. "Where was I? Ah yes. It seemed that Blue was on the far side of the clearing chasing rabbits, so who's ears was I scratching? I was afraid to look, but ever so slowly, I lowered my eyes. It was a baby bear, with its face in my pail eating up all my berries. I wasn't pleased, but the little guy was too small to be dangerous. Actually, he was kind of cute. Then I remembered. Never, ever get between a cub and his mama. Just then, the largest, scariest, meanest mama bear I ever saw poked its nose out of the brambles and headed right for me. What do you think I did?"

"Well, you still have Blue, so I guess the bear didn't eat him," said Robin.

"And you haven't climbed a tree since we were small," said Bolly Toadflax, his second cousin on his mother's side.

"You're not much of a runner, either," said Farmer Grubb. The old farmer had known Fibber since he was born.

"And that was a problem." Fibber considered whether scaling a tree or outrunning a bear would make a better story. "I flew up that ancient oak as if I had wings. I figure the lowest branch was twice my height, but I had both arms and legs wrapped around it, clinging for dear life, before I even knew I'd started to climb."

Farmer Grubb wiped tears of laughter from his eyes. "Alewife, pour him another round." The plump widow filled Fibber's tankard until the foam overflowed and ran down the side. The bitter smell of hops reached his nose. Life was good. The elderly farmer slapped Fibber on the back. "You told that story so well, I almost believed it." Fibber paused with the tankard halfway to his lips, unsure whether to be flattered or offended.

"Oh hey, look what I plowed up this morning." Robin held up something round and black with an oiled finish. The soil often yielded interesting things during the spring planting, like broken pottery, buttons, and bits of clay pipe. Fibber turned to look. It was an iron coin, larger than the coppers they used nowadays, and more finely made.

Bolly's eyes widened. "That's a goblin coin, the second one plowed up this year."

"There's no goblins in these parts," said Farmer Grubb.

"There used to be," said Bolly. "Some say, before decent people farmed these parts, this place was crawling with goblins."

"There's still a few goblins around. I use to court one," said Rusty Chubb. Robin scowled at him. "Oh sorry, I'm forgetting she's you're sister," said Rusty. Everyone laughed. Robin's sister had a sharp tongue, and she wasn't afraid to use it.

The hour grew late, and Missus Cowslip looked pointedly toward the door. Fibber and Robin were the last to get to their feet.

"Robin, you'll see him home, won't you?" said Missus Cowslip. Outside, the cold April air hit Fibber in the face and startled him awake. He hugged himself, shivering. The alewife shut the door behind them. Inside, the windows went dark one by one as the candles were snuffed out.

They followed the Great Road south, down a grassy slope and over the most prominent landmark near the village, the Stone Bridge. Fibber stopped at the highest part of the arch and looked down at the black water flowing beneath. The moon was almost full, its reflection bright against the glassy surface of the water except where its silver light vanished in the shadows of the marsh grasses on either bank. The river was no more than knee deep in places. It would be easy to wade across, yet whoever had built the bridge made it sturdy enough for an army to march across.

It was so peaceful here. Between the noisy confusion of family life and the hundreds of chores that make up a day of farming, Fibber seldom had a quiet moment to himself.

"Who do you think built this bridge?" Fibber asked Robin.

"It wasn't folks from here. We'd have just used rocks as stepping stones, or built something out of wood so a wagon could get across."

"It's said there's a great city to the south," said Fibber, "And another on the coast. Perhaps this road was built to connect them." Fibber stared into the water, thinking about how to use the idea in a story.

"Except we rarely see strangers on it," said Robin. "The folks that use it nowadays all live around here."

"Maybe it was built in ancient times. Maybe it was centuries old when the men from the sea swept through here and drove out the goblins," Fibber pronounced each syllable with care, as he'd had more to drink than he'd intended.

"Now you're making things up." Robin punched his arm. "C'mon Fibber, it's getting late. Stop looking at the water, nothing's going to happen down there."

Fibber let Robin lead him off the bridge. They traveled south along the Great Road, then turned off onto the farm lane which led to their houses. It was a walk of several miles through the forest to reach home and bed. It was dark in the woods, but the route was so familiar, he didn't need the light to find his way. A thick layer of fallen leaves blanketed the forest floor, absorbing all sound. Fibber couldn't even hear the river until it was close enough to touch.

They climbed the last ridge and descended into a hollow where a cluster of small farmsteads, a hamlet too small to have a name, was home to three families.

They were isolated here. To see other people or hear news of the outside world, Fibber had to hike several miles to the village across the Stone Bridge and spend time at the alehouse.

They arrived at the tiny cluster of cottages. The moon hung over the trees encircling their small fields. It was almost midnight, and every window in the hamlet was dark. The moon was bright enough to cast shadows, the outlines of tree branches black against the silver ground.

Robin saw Fibber to his front gate, "Goodnight, then. I'll see you tomorrow." He continued on to his own cottage next door.

Fibber stumbled across the yard, tripping over a hollow where the chickens scratched during the day. He shouldn't have drunk so much, but people had liked his stories particularly well this evening and had kept filling is tankard. He lifted the cowhide flap that covered the door to their cottage and tripped over the threshold. He froze, waiting for Blue to raise a ruckus and wake the whole family, but the old hound just thumped his tail lightly.

The kitchen fire had been banked long ago, but a few coals still glowed orange-red. Their warmth filled the small room. Moonlight washed over the earthen floor. Its gray-blue light fell across the pallets where his younger children slept, as well as the cot for his oldest son Tom. A smudge of shadow revealed the cradle beside the bed he shared with his wife. She snored softly, but not enough to wake the baby draped across her chest.

Fibber crossed the room with careful steps, feeling his way across the hard packed floor with his toes. He'd almost reached the bed without waking anyone when he tripped over the empty cradle and sent it crashing against the wall. "Plague and drought!" he cursed, hopping around on his non-stubbed foot. From the safety of his mother's arms, the baby drew a breath that seemed to go on forever, then let out an enormous shriek.

"Fibber, is that you?" Rosie's voice was thick with sleep. He struggled to hear her above the baby's wails. "How many rounds of ale did you have?"

"Jush two. Ah ain't drunk," said Fibber. He stripped off his

5

clothes and dropped them on the floor unfolded, then fell back against the pillow. The room spun. He clutched the sides of the bed and felt like he was dropping like a stone.

Chapter 2

Lost Pig

ibber woke to full daylight. Usually, when he stepped outside in the morning, the eastern sky was streaked with orange and gold. Today, if there'd been a sunrise he'd have enjoyed seeing, he'd just missed it. He felt a twinge of regret, as well as a tug of shame for having drunk more than he'd meant to. Again.

Fibber stumbled back from the privy, his head pounding. He leaned against the withy fence around the pigpen and rested for a moment before going into the cottage. He bent over, waiting to be sick. Nothing happened. The bad thing about not being sick was that he still felt terrible. He splashed water on his face from the stone trough for the livestock. Looking to see that he was unobserved, he cupped his hands and drank the water meant for the cow. It was cold and sweet. He smoothed his hair with wet hands and went inside.

"Fibber, what took you so long? Did you milk the cow?" Rosie bent over the fire pit to stir something in the iron pot.

"Yes, Love."

"Can you pour a measure of milk into the oatmeal? It's almost ready."

"Oh, I meant to say, I was about to milk the cow. I'll do it right now." His cheeks burned. He hurried to the barn and returned with a pail filled almost to the rim, because he'd forgotten to milk the cow the night before.

One of the neighbors chose that moment to start hammering. Each blow made its way deep into Fibber's skull.

Fibber looked around for the culprit. Next door, Robin was lugging a pail of milk from the barn to the house. It wasn't him.

A ladder leaned against the side of the house just across from Fibber's front gate. His neighbor, Thierry Fairbairn, was on the roof hammering shingles into place. Thierry's small daughter climbed the ladder with a few slates in her hand, gave them to him, and went down for more. The pile of slates was taller than she was. It looked like the hammering would go on all day. Fibber wondered if his head might actually explode.

Rosie stood by the pigpen, pacing back and forth.

"Fibber, the pig got loose." There were tears in her voice. The pig was half their wealth, and without her, they wouldn't have enough to eat next winter. "We can't afford to lose her, Fibber. I can't imagine a worse disaster."

Fibber stiffened. "I'm sure I closed the gate. I remembered to check it when I came in last night after you were asleep, and I'm sure..."

"She didn't get out by the gate." Rosie pointed to a hole in the base of the withy fence. "She found a gap and pushed her way out. What are we going to do?" Rosie stood there wringing her hands. She looked frightened.

Fibber gathered her up in his arms. "Don't worry, Love, we'll get her back. Remember last fall, when we found her in the acorn grove. Pigs love acorns. I'll take Tom, and we'll go there first to look for her." Fibber turned toward the house. "Tom! Bring a halter for the pig."

Tom appeared from around the back of the house. He was a slender youth, but easily his father's height. He held a rope in his hand, fashioned into a makeshift halter.

Fibber and Tom headed for the acorn grove, miles away and on the other side of the Great Road. They set out on the narrow lane. Beyond the clearings of their neighbors' fields, the trees closed in on both sides. Where the lane ran along the edge of the river, sunlight sparkled on the water's surface, visible between the saplings that grew on its banks. They left the river behind, and the trees pressed in around them. All sound was muffled, and the light was green and dim.

They passed through a sunny patch where cow parsley grew on the sandy bank on either side of the path. A bee bobbed on one of the stems, its white flowers not fully opened in the morning chill. Fibber looked more closely. It wasn't a bee, it was a yellow jacket. Irritable and aggressive, they were nothing like the gentle honeybees he kept in straw hives at the back of the garden.

As Fibber watched, half a dozen yellow jackets crawled from an unseen tunnel that led to their nest at the edge of the lane. A muffled humming reached him, almost below hearing.

"Stay back." Fibber motioned Tom away.

Fibber led Tom around the yellow jackets. They struggled through the bracken until the buzzing sound was well behind them and Fibber judged it safe to return to the path.

"We're lucky we ran into them first thing in the morning. They're not so bad now because it's cold, but come afternoon, they'll be something terrible," Fibber said.

A short distance beyond the yellow jacket nest, the trees thinned. Fibber and Tom stepped onto the Great Road. Fibber looked at the sky, frowning.

"Tom, what do you think of those clouds? They're sort of greenish, and they're moving way too fast. It's unnatural."

"If it was late in a midsummer's afternoon with a thunderstorm brewing, you'd think nothing of it," said Tom. "It's just early in the season for this sort of weather, that's all."

Fibber walked to the middle of the road, the gravel crunching under his feet. He stretched his arms as wide as he could. It would have taken three of him to reach across its width.

"Tom," asked Fibber, "Have you ever wondered why this road was built?"

"I never thought about it going anywhere," said Tom. "I haven't taken it more than four or five miles in either direction."

Fibber studied the wide boulevard as if he'd never seen it before. It was well made and more than wide enough for the small amount of traffic that used it now. The roadbed was level and flat, although somewhat neglected. Here and there, wildflowers sprang from its stony surface. White clouds of cow parsley and thick-stemmed crosswort grew knee-high in the middle of the road, and sow thistles, with blossoms like small sunflowers, reached to his hip.

Far down the Great Road, to the south, a colossal plume of dust blocked part of the horizon. It looked like something large was on the move, maybe a whole herd of cattle. Now that would be a sight to see. But enough of that, he had a pig to find.

Fibber slapped his forehead. "I forgot to look for the pig the woods around the house before we set out."

"Well, last time she got out, we found her in the acorn grove. She's probably there now," said Tom.

Fibber worked out what to do. "Tell you what. I'll press on ahead to the grove, and you look in the woods near the house. Remember to steer clear of the yellow jackets."

"Yes, Dad," Tom nodded. Her turned around and jogged down the lane back toward their farm. After he disappeared among the trees, Fibber crossed the Great Road to the path which led to the acorn grove.

Fibber didn't travel down this path very often. It was on the wrong side of the Great Road, and it took him further from home than he liked to go.

Fibber walked for miles. He kept thinking he'd almost reached the grove, and he kept being wrong. He was ready to turn back, when there it was. Oak trees closed in on all sides, and last year's acorns lay so thick on the ground, the woodland animals hadn't been able to eat them all.

Unfortunately, the pig wasn't there. Fibber's shoulders sagged. He wasn't familiar with this part of the forest and didn't know where to look next. There were lots of woods to search and little chance of finding the pig before nightfall. Dusk would come early today, what with that strange overcast. Discouraged, he turned around and began the long hike back. With any luck, Tom had already found the pig near their house.

Fibber had been trudging for almost an hour, stumbling over tree roots and loose rocks. The trees started to thin, a sign that the Great Road lay just ahead. And on the other side was the farm lane leading to his cottage. Fibber picked up his pace.

Chapter 3

The Black Army

A deep vibration traveled through the ground. It felt like drumbeats or distant thunder. The wind stirred. It carried with it an overwhelmingly musky odor. Fibber rounded the last bend. The Great Road lay twenty feet ahead. He emerged from the trees, and his jaw dropped.

Rank upon rank of monstrous creatures marched up the road, ten or twelve abreast, spilling over onto the shoulder on each side. They weren't human. Their skin was greenish gray and their features mutilated. Teeth like fangs protruded from misshapen lips, and many of them were hunchbacked. *Goblins!* Last night, Fibber had held a goblin coin in his hand, a relic from ancient times. No goblin had been spotted around here in living memory, and there was no mention of them in the local family histories.

Fibber dropped to his belly and crawled through the grass, then peered at the road from behind a clump of saplings.

The goblins continued to march by. One wore a necklace of teeth, and the unhealthy-looking skin of its face was pierced with gold rings that stretched its cheeks out of shape. The horrible thing looked at him, and their eyes locked. It nudged its neighbor and pointed. The other one noticed Fibber and laughed. Fibber's throat tightened.

Hugging the ground as closely as possible, Fibber crawled backwards and melted into the tall grasses like a rabbit avoiding a wolf. The safety of the woods was a stone's throw behind him, but he didn't think he could make it. However, the monstrous creatures took no further interest in him, continuing to march without breaking rank. Apparently, they didn't kill gawkers on the side of the road.

The column stretched into the south like a colossal trail of ants, black and glittering. Here and there, standards rose above the troops, many of them unraveling at the bottom and soiled with the dust of the road. The column seemed to have no end. It disappeared behind the rise of a hill. Against the horizon, a plume of dust raised by countless boots rose high in the air.

That dreadful column blocked Fibber's way back to Rosie and the children. He could flee into the safety of the forest, but he wasn't willing to abandon his family.

The column marched on, driven by a relentless drumbeat. Each goblin was encased in leather armor, black or dark brown in color, and reinforced with scales or metal plates. Gray or brown fabric showed beneath the armor under the arms or where the pieces met. Each of the dark-garbed warriors brandished a spear or cudgel of some sort. Most carried shields painted with harsh-looking designs.

If the creatures continued on their current path, they would cross the Stone Bridge and enter the settled places where families made their homes. *Oh please, oh please just let them be passing through on their way to somewhere else. Just leave us alone.*

"Hail Zuriel!" they chanted in time with the drum.

Zuriel. That must be their leader. The battle cry echoed down the line, the sound ancient and evil. It chilled Fibber's blood.

A group of horsemen rode by, ringed by a guard of goblins who were taller and wore more elaborate armor than the others.

Behind the horsemen was the largest standard Fibber had ever seen. Against the black background, it bore an angular, sharp-edged design, the forced marriage of the symbol for Earth with the symbol for Fire. The fabric had faded in the sun, and loose threads hung from its edges.

The goblin army marched by for another hour. Around midday, the baggage wagons trundled by, bringing up the rear.

They disappeared into the woods to the north and left the Great Road deserted. A cloud of dust hung in the air.

Fibber climbed down the embankment and stood in the center of the road. Not a single wildflower remained standing, and the grass on either side was flattened and dead. The road itself was torn up, rutted by wagon wheels and fouled with the droppings of their animals. He hoped it was their animals.

Fibber left the road and took off toward his cottage. Where was Tom? Was his family safe? He had to reach them.

He made it as far as the place where the path almost touched the river when a stitch in his side forced him to stop. He held his side, panting. Through a screen of saplings, the sun sparkled on the river, and waves slapped against the rocks. His farmstead was over the hill and down in the hollow beyond, half a mile further on.

Tom ambled down the hill. "Dad? No luck?"

"We have to get home. I have to know that your mother is safe," said Fibber, breathing hard.

"Of course she's safe, I just saw her. I went to the house, but the pig hasn't come back on her own yet. I wouldn't either, what with Thierry hammering on the roof all day."

Fibber tilted his head to listen, but he didn't hear any hammering. "Never mind that, an enormous band of goblins is marching toward the Stone Bridge. They're headed for the alehouse and the farmsteads around it." Fibber pushed between the saplings that grew on the riverbank and pointed to the Stone Bridge. Even though the footpath to the village was long and winding, the bridge was only a quarter of a mile upriver. Fibber squinted to see. At the center of the arch, two boys dangled fishing poles over the side of the stone railing.

Tom's face was still. "Does this have a punch line?"

Fibber grabbed him by the arm. "Go back to the house. Take your mother and the children into the root cellar. Warn the neighbors, too." Tom shrugged, then trotted off in the direction of the farmstead.

After Tom left, Fibber stared at the bridge with horrified fascination, unable to tear himself away.

Chapter 4

The Pale Warriors

ibber stood frozen on the riverbank, listening. A long warbling song was interrupted by the scolding of a jay. The wind picked up, and a heavy overcast blocked the sun. Other sounds reached him from across the water, faint and far away, a deep pounding rumble and the pulse of drums.

The boys dropped their poles and fled, heading up the slope at a dead run.

A handful of dark-colored goblins reached the bridge and raced across it, cresting the center arch and going down the other side. The main body of the army followed close behind, moving more slowly. Ragged black standards swung above their heads. Large numbers of them broke off from the host and waded into the river itself, splashing through the shallows and jumping from rock to rock.

Opposite, on the slope below the alehouse, another army had massed. Their clothing was pale in color, and their armor glinted silver in the noonday sun. Pennants floated over their heads, the blues and purples of wildflowers.

The wind lifted a banner, revealing a ship on a blue background. *Not the colors of wildflowers, the colors of the sea.* Like everyone else from around here, Fibber grew up on legends of the warriors from the sea who'd arrived in their great oceangoing ships and had driven out the goblins. Fibber blinked and looked again, not believing what he saw. He told fantastical stories, he wasn't supposed to be in them.

A trumpet sounded. A handful of pale soldiers rushed toward the bridge. They reached it just as the first of the goblins finished crossing. The pale soldiers fought to hold them back, but the goblins kept coming. At the same time, more and more of the dark-colored creatures scrambled up the riverbank, waterlogged clothing plastered to their legs.

A hail of arrows sailed through the air from the goblin side, and the pale soldiers raised their shields. Arrows struck the wood with a dull thud. A long line of the pale warriors advanced down the hill. A longer and thicker line of goblins marched up to meet them. The distance between the two lines closed. They collided with a crash. The din of combat carried across the water and reached Fibber a quarter mile away from his vantage point among the saplings.

The goblins forced men from the sea back up the hill, and their formerly straight line wavered and threatened to break under the goblin assault. It looked like they were being overwhelmed. Then quite unexpectedly, the enemy line frayed at the ends, then crumbled and fell apart.

All at once, goblins bolted for the river. They raced across the bridge and splashed through the shallow water beneath it, trying to flee in the direction they'd come. A wave of pale soldiers pursued them. Soon there wasn't a living goblin on either side of the river. Bodies lay scattered on the ground and in the chilly water.

Fibber abandoned his lookout place in the saplings. He had to know that his family was safe. He took a step toward the farmstead, and then hesitated. If he missed seeing the retreat, he wouldn't be able to tell the story. He danced with indecision, then turned around and ran down the lane.

A mile later, he reached the Great Road. The clang of metal on metal filled the air. Someone howled, and someone else cursed. The trees had not yet leafed out. Between their trunks, he could see something of the skirmish.

Fibber moved from tree to tree, using the underbrush as cover. Where the trees gave way to meadow, he dropped to his stomach. He crawled as far as he dared, then parted the tall grasses and lifted his head.

The goblins were running, dropping their weapons, and tripping over the bodies of the dead as the pale warriors pursued them. Pennants of blue and green floated from the tips of the pale warriors' lances, and their swords shown like mirrors. Each swing of a weapon raised a spray of black blood which splashed their silver armor. The foot soldiers wielded spears with silvery tips. Each thrust left a smear of black blood up the shaft. Fibber's stomach twisted.

In the midst of the chaos, half a dozen horsemen rode south. Their mounts were black, and so was their clothing and armor. They rode behind a standard that was frayed and pale with dust. Fibber had seen it before, a fusion of the symbols for Fire and Earth.

A wedge-shaped formation of men on pale horses cantered around the bend, led by a tall, broad-shouldered man. He rode a white stallion that must have been at least sixteen hands tall. His standard bearer carried the banner of a ship under full sail, the emblem of the warriors from the sea. The tall man must be their leader.

One of the pale warriors stood in his stirrups and pointed at the black horsemen. "General Olwen! That's him! That's Lord Zuriel!"

A trumpet pealed, and hoofbeats thundered against the earth. General Olwen spurred his stallion to a gallop and bore down on the retreating enemy, his men right behind him. The dark horsemen spurred their mounts and galloped down the road. The pale warriors had almost overtaken them when the tall one, Fibber guessed it was Lord Zuriel, wheeled to face them. He advanced in slow, menacing steps, and his sword emerged from the scabbard with a hiss.

The pale horses danced around and tossed their heads, whinnying, as their riders fought for control. Only the General's horse remained still, beyond a twitch that ran up its haunches.

The leaders locked eyes, their bodies tense, poised to strike. Fibber was reminded of two dogs circling one another, their fangs bared. Their men watched in silence, waiting to see what would happen.

Lord Zuriel was the first to speak. His voice was low and harsh. General Olwen stiffened, and his mouth formed a thin line. Whatever was said must have been an insult, because General Olwen's fingers tightened on the hilt of his sword. One of his men laid a hand on the General's arm, but he shook it off.

Something moved at the edge of Fibber's vision. On the far side of the road, a goblin archer knelt on a spur of rock. He notched a barbed arrow and drew it back to his cheek. Now he was sighting along the shaft, about to loose it.

Do something. Warn them, create a distraction. Fibber felt in his pocket for the sling he always carried. The goblin archer was too far away to hit, but maybe he could make a sound to warn the pale warriors. He looked around for a target that would make a noise. Anything metal would do, a helmet, a shield, the breastplate of a soldier.

But before Fibber could act, the goblin archer shrieked and tumbled from the rock, his hands clutching the shaft of an arrow lodged in his throat. He hit the dirt with a thud and lay face down, black blood soaking the ground beneath him. The shaft had snapped when he hit. The feathered end, a mass of ragged wooden splinters, lay beside the body. Fibber's breakfast rose to his throat.

The two armies continued to flow down the Great Road, the goblins fleeing, the warriors pursuing them. A great press of pale warriors built up behind General Olwen, while the goblins melted away.

Lord Zuriel advanced on the General and raised his sword.

The General laughed. "Look behind you."

Lord Zuriel's head snapped around, apparently realizing for the first time that his army had left without him.

Pale soldiers surrounded him. Lord Zuriel fought hard but was quickly overwhelmed. Just before they pulled him from the saddle, he made a gesture at General Olwen that couldn't have been considered polite. A mob of soldiers pressed around the spot where he hit the ground. Nearby, his horse wandered riderless, the saddle empty.

Warriors fell upon the few remaining goblins like a wall of destruction. They dismounted and advanced with their swords drawn. The goblins recoiled in terror. One dropped his weapon. Another tripped over it and went down hard. In an instant, the pale warriors surrounded the goblin on the ground and hacked him to pieces. Fibber had seen enough. He backed away as quietly as he could, hoping desperately that he could get away without being caught.

Chapter 5

You'll Never Believe It

Fibber moved quietly along the path. The sun had come out again, warming the afternoon air. Away from the road, the sounds of skirmishing were somewhat muffled, but he could still see some of the fighting through the trees.

A pale soldier advanced on a group of goblins. He swung his weapon. One of the goblins screamed and fell to the ground. Its two companions fled the Great Road and dove into the farm lane, heading directly for Fibber. Fibber hid in the underbrush, holding his breath and hoping they'd run by without seeing him.

My family's at the end of this lane. Fibber's mouth went dry. He had to stop them. He took a deep breath to steady himself, then drew the sling from his pocket. With his eyes fastened on the goblins, he felt around in the sandy soil for a smooth rock. Just when he feared he'd run out of time, his fingers closed on a nice heavy one. He fitted it to the pouch of the sling, then swung it once, twice, and released it. But the range was too great. It struck a tree behind the lead goblin. The next stone he found was larger than the first. It didn't fit in the sling, but it didn't matter. The goblins were closing in too fast. He didn't have time to make the shot.

There was a humming nearby. Something stung him on the knuckle. Yellow jackets, active and excitable now that the day had grown warm. They were thickest on the ground just above the entrance to their nest, uncomfortably close to Fibber's hiding place. He would use the weapons he had. Bracing himself for what was to come, he hurled the stone against the nest as hard as he could.

A cloud of yellow jackets rose up in the air, angry and venomous. They stung him again and again, but he didn't cry out. He didn't dare. The goblins would kill him if they found him.

The lead goblin stopped in his tracks. He hopped up and down, flapping his arms in pain, then ran backwards to get away. He crashed into the second goblin and knocked him down. The second goblin was on his feet in an instant, racing after his companion. Both were screaming something that was probably goblin for, "Bees, bees, I hate bees!" Apparently they were more afraid of the yellow jackets than of the pale warriors waiting for them on the Great Road.

Over a mile later, Fibber reached his house with one eye swollen shut, his chest heaving, and his hair glued to his forehead with sweat. The little ones were playing in the garden. One had uprooted a daylily and was hitting his sister with the stalk. In the neighboring field, Robin walked behind a plow. No one had gone to the root cellar.

Tom was working in the kitchen garden. He put down his hoe. "Guess what, Dad? Robin found our pig in his orchard and brought her back. She was already safe in her pen when I got here." He pointed to the pigpen, where the pig grunted over a pail of cabbage leaves.

Fibber staggered into the cottage. Inside, Rosie balanced the baby on one hip while she stirred something on the fire with her free hand. The room smelled of chicken broth and warm bread.

"Rosie Love, you won't believe what I saw. A horde of goblins came up the Great Road and tried to cross the Stone Bridge," he began, unable to contain his excitement.

She narrowed her eyes.

"But an army of pale warriors, the men from the sea, came from the other direction and drove them back."

Rosie's face was still. "And I suppose Tom saw it too?"

Tom stiffened. He looked from his father's face to his mother's and back. "Oh hey, I'd better repair the withy fence before the pig gets out again." He shot across the room at more than his usual relaxed pace. The cowhide flap dropped shut behind him.

Rosie shook her head and turned back to the hearth. "Really, Fibber? You can't do better than that?"

About the Author

Liz Hayes is an engineer by inclination and training. She began her career at Jet Propulsion Labs, and later moved east to be an analyst and statistician for the Federal Government.

She's fascinated by medieval reenactment, and writes LOTR fanfiction under the penname Uvatha the Horseman. While doing the research for a fanfic about Sauron forging the Ring, she joined the local guild and became an amateur blacksmith herself. It's an excellent hobby which combines her two favorite things, craft projects and pyromania.

She lives in Northern Virginia with her husband and three teenage children she keeps in line by threatening to show up at PTA meetings in full Jedi robes.